BOY WANTS PET

For Mark, with love L.R.
For Laura, Grace and Oscar L.W.

First published in hardback in 2010 by Hodder Children's Books

Hodder Children's Books
338 Euston Road, London, NW1 3BH

Hodder Children's Books Australia
Level 17/207 Kent Street, Sydney, NSW 2000

A catalogue record of this book is available from the British Library.

ISBN: 978 0 340 98838 1
10 9 8 7 6 5 4 3 2 1

Printed in China

Hodder Children's Books is a division of Hachette Children's Books
An Hachette UK Company
www.hachette.co.uk

www.leewildish.com

www.lynnerickards.co.uk

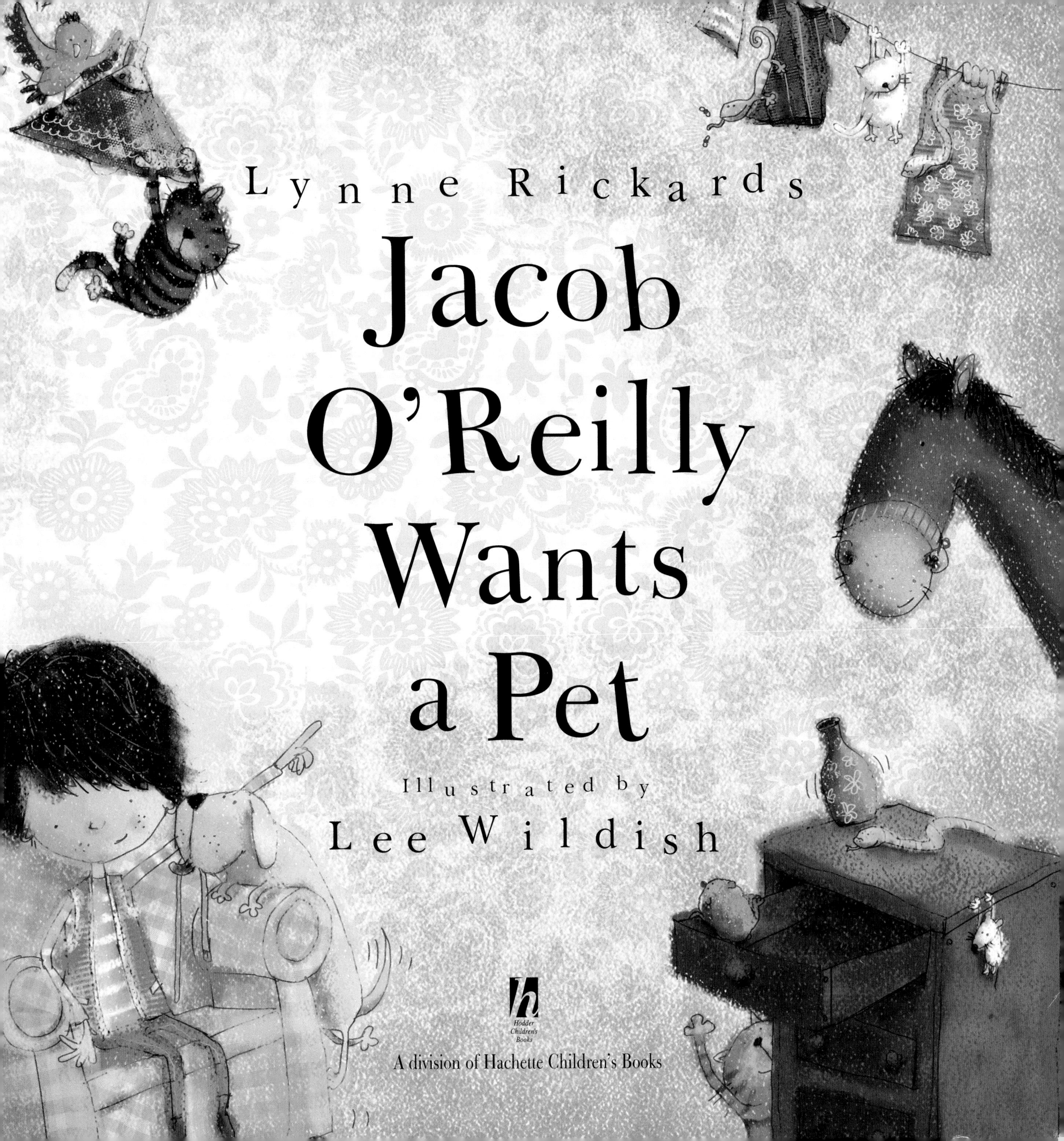

Lynne Rickards

Jacob O'Reilly Wants a Pet

Illustrated by
Lee Wildish

Hodder Children's Books
A division of Hachette Children's Books

Jacob O'Reilly had tried all he could
to convince Mum and Dad he'd be ever so good –
an absolute angel, the greatest son yet –
if only they'd let him have
one little pet!

I want a pet! please x
NUMBER
1
SON

UNITED WIN AGAIN!
DAILY GOSSIP

He asked for a **dog** but Dad didn't want fleas.
He tried for a **cat** but the fur made Mum sneeze.

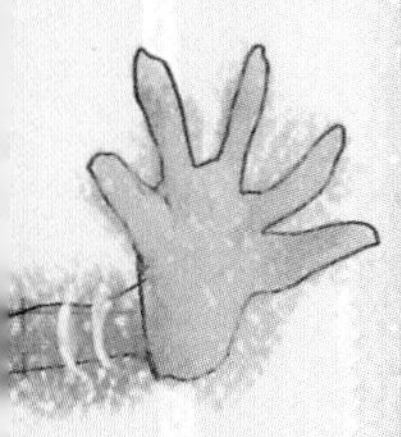

He went through a list of small **rodents** for sale,
but the very idea turned Mum and Dad pale.

'If I'm not allowed **gerbils**
or **hamsters** or **mice**,
don't you think an **iguana**
would be rather nice?

He'd be awfully quiet
and eat all the bugs,
and never leave fur or dead
birds on the rugs...

Oh, **PLEASE** can I have a pet?'

'An emu can make
a fine pet, have you heard?
It is said to be quite an affectionate bird,
and although it is tall and needs quite a large nest,
it keeps to itself and is never a pest...
Oh, **PLEASE** can I have a pet?'

'A **walrus** would be an ideal sort of pet.
He could live in the bathtub to keep himself wet.
I'd comb out his whiskers and scrub his broad back,
and brush those big tusks when he finished a snack...

Oh, **PLEASE** can I have a pet?'

Well, Mum and Dad thought about all these suggestions while waiting for Jacob to run out of questions.

They pondered their choices and finally said, 'Why not try your own pet-sitting business instead?'

AARDVARK
HORSE
COW
PIG
DONKEY
TIGER
CAT
DOG
SNAKE
GRIFFIN
DRAGON
SHEEP
HAMSTER
MOUSE
RAT
LIZARD
STICK INSECT
SPIDER
LION
ZEBRA
ANT NEST
KANGAROO
CHIMPMONK
ELEPHANT
MONKEY
GUINEA PIG
SLIMY BUGS
GRASSHOPPER
ANTEATER
DINOSAUR
Please can I have

The very next day, Jacob put up a sign:
'Come one and come all! Any number is fine!
I'll care for your pets while you take a nice break.
They'll have a great time here with
Pet-Sitter Jake!'

6

In no time at all Jacob
had a full house –
four dogs and
five hamsters,
six cats and one
mouse...

DIARY
of
Jacob
DO NOT
TOUCH

A python called
Morris lay curled
on his bed,

two donkeys, five
sheep and one
horse filled the shed,

the kitchen was hopping
with **rabbits** and **hares**,

and somebody's **zebra**
was blocking the stairs.

At feeding time Jacob was run off his feet –
some pets wanted salad, and some wanted meat.
They needed a hose-down when dinner was done,
and then it was time for a **marathon run!**

When two weeks were up and the owners came back,
The house had turned into a flea-bitten shack.
The minute the last pet whizzed off into town,
Pet-Sitter Jake went and pulled his sign down!

SH33P1
FRAGILE
THIS WAY UP

And that's when he noticed a rather fine **snail**,
Just sitting contentedly there on a nail.
'Hello, there,' smiled Jacob, 'I don't think we've met.'
And finally Jacob had **found the right pet!**

Fetch!
!
5
FINISH
DOG